THEN JUDGMENT

...the three days Jesus did not spend in the tomb

CARYL MCADOO

Praying my story gives God glory!

This book is a work of fiction. Any references to historical events, real people, or real places are used fictitiously. Other names, places, characters, and events are products of the author's imaginations, and any resemblance to actual events or places or persons, living or dead, is entirely coincidental.

First Edition April 8, 2022
Peaceable Publishing
Printed and bound in the United States of America

IBSN 9798-4203-218-43
Also available as eBook AISN B09SJ5GD7F
Coming soon in Large Print and Audio!

Cover art by Randi Gammons Graphic Design
https://randigammonsdesigns.myportfolio.com/

For author to speak, contact:
Peaceable Publishing
Post Office Box 622
Clarksville, Texas 75426

DEDICATION

Oh, the love of the Lord is great! With my whole heart, I desire to serve and bring Him glory!

I dedicate this story to God's unfathomable Love—a Love so deep that He literally sacrificed His beloved only begotten Son.to afford me the opportunity to be with Him eternally.

And I was a wretch, y'all! As a mother, I can't imagine sacrificing one of my three sons to save anybody, much less a derelict pagan!

The next great love of my life is my husband!

What a gift God gave me in Ron McAdoo! I also dedicate this book to the one who loves me like Christ loves the church! My c0-author (even though his name is not on the covers—by his choice). I know I do not deserve him, but am so blessed to say I am his and he is mine!

My Ladies' Monday Mornin' Bible Study group!

I dedicate this book to these ladies who I love, too! We meet weekly to study God's Word at the Double R Cowboy Church in Clarksville. They've accepted me and loved me in spite of myself even though I'm not a member of their congregation: Edna DePriest, Kristin Carmack, Shirley Williams, Cheryl Sims, Susan Ahlmeyer and her granddaughter Rhe, Darla Childeress, Betty Wolfe, Clara Phillips, Lorri Mikelich, and Kathy Moss. I hope my brain hasn't left anyone out.

AND AS IT IS APPOINTED
UNTO MEN ONCE TO DIE, BUT
AFTER THIS THE JUDGMENT:

HEBREWS 9:27

$\mathcal{A}$CKNOWLEDGEMENTS

~~God~~ my Creator and the the Lover of my soul!

~~Ron~~my husband who loves me like Christ loves the church!

~~ My helpers~~All those who help me get my stories to market in their best possible form to bless His Kingdom are great blessings from the Lord!

Lenda Selph, my sweetest sister-friend I love with my whole heart! She only lives about forty-five minutes away and we nenver let too much time go by without getting together for a meal! What a great cook and hostess she is! She's proofed every book!

Cass Wessel, my dear Pennsylvania sister who I met in 2013 at the ACFW Conference in Indianapolis! Hard to believe we've known each other almost ten years now!

Debbey Cozzone, my Tennessee sister! God has bound our hearts together! I got to meet her face-to-face at a Wendy's on the Interstate when she was coming into Texas to see her new grandsugar!

Susan Johnson and Joy Gibson have been supporters since the beginning of my Indie career in 2015! ARC readers who catch an uh-oh now and then!

Alice Kimes and Kristin Carmack, two relatively new readers I met online at one of my Facebook parties, do too! Kristin only lives twenty minutes away, so we get together as often as we can.

Miss Randi Gammons designs my beautiful covers! I'm so grateful for her—a gift from God!

~~My readers~~whose faithful and continued support keeps me writing! I am grateful for reviews and every time any of my series or titles are recommended! BLESSINGS, y'all!

How is One Saved?

For God so loved the world, that he gave his only begotten Son, that whosoever believeth in him should not perish, but have everlasting life. For God sent not his Son into the world to condemn the world; but that the world through him might be saved. John 3:16-17

He that believeth and is baptized shall be saved; but he that believeth not shall be damned. Mark 16:16

And they [Paul and Silas when miraculously released from prison, but they stayed put] said, Believe on the Lord Jesus Christ, and thou shalt be saved, and thy house. Acts 16:31

That if thou shalt confess with thy mouth the Lord Jesus, and shalt believe in thine heart that God hath raised him from the dead, thou shalt be saved. Romans 10:9

For by grace are ye saved through faith; and that not of yourselves: it is the gift of God: Not of works, lest any man should boast. Ephesians 2:8

CHAPTER ONE

Dodi's new charges stood in a straight line before him. He strolled along assessing each angel. A few he knew from the pitch or a game of rocks, but he'd have to learn the names of most.

Never in a star's life would he ever have dreamed he'd be given a legion to command. Imagine . . . Commander over sixty centurions, each over a hundred . . . more honor than he ever deserved.

A brother of the host—he had yet to hear the angel's name—pointed a wing tip skyward. "Sir."

Raising his gaze, Dodi watched one of the triplets circle overhead. The magnificent servant of God dove straight for him. It had to be Gabriel, but why?

The archangel landed, but only folded his wings halfway, as though not staying long. "Dodi, you are needed. Come with me."

"Yes, of course. Where am I needed, sir?"

"We fly to the throne of the Lord God Almighty. Come."

Love flowed over him as a wave onto the shore of the Crystal Sea. The throne room! God's presence! He treasured nothing more! He brought his wingtip to his chest.

"All glory be to Him Who sits on the throne! Blessed be the name of the Lord! I am ready to serve. What a blessing to be summoned by God Himself."

To keep up with the archangel's speed, he beat his wings double time, and the great angel was not even flying full feather! Only Gabriel's brothers could fly as fast as God's messenger.

Coming upon the outskirts of the Great I Am's manifest presence, the taller angel—by a full head, maybe a bit more—landed, turned backwards, then spread his wings, an impressive breadth.

"Remain beneath me in my shadow until I speak otherwise."

"I will." Dodi wanted to tell the great angel that he could stand on his feet in God's glory longer than most, but Gabriel . . .

He could remain stand in God's presence for all eternity if need be.

Oh, the glory!

Even at the edge and though being shaded, God's splendor permeated Dodi. As always, it was wonderful! Nothing better existed!

Once inside, great rolling thunderings and the cherubim's repeated cries of holiness to the Lord reached his ears. At that distance though, they sounded only as a whisper.

Around the archangel's wings, flashes of multicolored lights darted and danced. The praises and blessings bestowed upon the Almighty increased in volume the nearer he walked.

What an awesome God he served!

Strolling in the archangel's shadow, he longed to prostrate himself and bathe fully in God's glory, but . . . the Creator bade him come, and he must show himself to the Lord.

After thousands of wholly enjoyable steps, Gabriel folded his wings and moved aside.

"Glory! Power! Honor! Praise be unto You Who created all that is! Blessings, Master!" He swooned a bit and knelt on one knee. "I am at Your holy service, my Lord."

FLY WITH YOUR THOUSANDS TO ISRAEL

The pure love emanating from the One and Only true God filled Dodi to the utmost. He basked in His glorious peace. Israel. On His world that circled fourth from the sun, just below the second heaven?

Why would the Creator need him there?

Though he would think leaving the third heaven would be odious, with all of his being, at God's Word, Dodi desired only to be in the land of Abraham and his descendants.

Obedience showed his absolute love for the Great God Who sat on the throne!

WHAT MUST BE SHALL BE REVEALED

Once again, Gabriel spread his wings and shadowed Dodi. The mighty archangel sang twelve notes then whistled three more.

"That tune, contrary to what your eyes tell you, is a direct route to Nazareth. Now fly, friend. Gather your thousands and be on your way. My brothers' legions mass over the Dead Sea."

Never had Dodi flown from God's manifest presence. Only by being shielded could he still stand, leaving the Almighty's throne.

No matter how hard he pulled, he remained in Gabriel's shadow until he crossed the visible line then flew high above over the Crystal Sea.

Finally over his charges, who patiently waited in formation, he whistled them aloft then sang the portal open. Amazingly enough, he led his thousands directly to the portal over Nazareth using the archangel's song.

He grinned. Gabriel had been right. Dodi would never have believed his eyes. Coming into the light of the earth's star, the Most High charged him.

PROTECT MARY TO THE LAST FEATHER

How could it be? Dodi never before heard the Lord speak directly to his heart.

Not only had He spoken to him but revealed in a star's twinkle exactly where this maiden resided and her appearance. He suddenly could hardly wait to be in the earthling's presence and protect her from all evil.

Though why, he knew not—other than God commanded it. For some reason, the woman needed his safeguarding.

What an honor the Lord chose to shower on his unworthy head!

As the days and weeks of earth spent themselves, it surprised Dodi that Mary was found to be with child. Her intended, Joseph—a very good and righteous fellow—chose to put her way privily, and Mary wept.

The next day, the man changed his mind.

It puzzled him why the man would do either. The betrothed's actions made little sense—put her away and then take her back. Yet . . . Dodi knew it to be God's will.

In the fullness of time, due to Rome's decree that all were to be taxed in the place of their birth, Joseph took Mary, then heavy with child, to Bethlehem.

Upon their arrival, Dodi hated that the only room to be had was in the animals' stalls. In short order, Mary was delivered of her baby, a man-child.

How puzzling. Michael and two of his legions showed themselves in the heavens and sang God's praises above nearby meadows where shepherds watched over their flocks.

"Glory! Glory to God in the highest!"
NEVER LEAVE THE CHILD
MY ONLY BEGOTTEN SON
PROTECT HIM UNTIL THE FULLNESS OF TIME
 God's very Own? His only begotten Son?

How could it be?

Yet with the Great I Am all things were certainly possible. No wonder the Lord wanted the young lady guarded to the last feather!

Glory bumps waved over his flesh, realizing just how great the honor bestowed upon him proved. He studied the swaddled Babe . . . His face . . . His eyes. The Son! Hallelujah!

God become man yet still fully God! He positioned his thousands! No harm would come near his Master!

Spreading the fear of losing his power, Lucifer stirred King Herod to slay the newborn King of Israel. In a dream, however, Dodi was allowed to see, God warned Joseph to flee to Egypt with Mary and the Child.

A third of Dodi's legion went ahead of the holy family, a third surrounded them, and the last third as their rearguard.

It hurt Dodi's heart to witness the merciless slaughter of young boys. How could a king bestow such evil on his own people?

Didn't Herod know he could not stop God from fulfilling His plan—whatever that might be?

And Lucifer! How could the most beautiful archangel think he could do such a thing as thwart the everlasting

God? Kill His only begotten Son! His pride had ruined him.

To kill, steal, and destroy all that he could had become the last-created angel's sole mission. He sought to achieve the perversion of every holy thing of God in the earth.

Besides deceiving and manipulating those angels of the hosts foolish enough to follow his rebellion against the Most High—using them for his malevolent purpose—he sourced the hands of evil men for his dirty work.

He first coerced them into his wickedness then accused them of failing their Creator, suffocating them in guilt and his condemnation.

What an evil and loathsome creature he'd become.

Once Herod slept with the kings of men who passed before him, the Almighty called His Son out of Egypt to the town of Nazareth. Dodi flew ever in sight of his beloved Master.

As if just another Jewish boy, Jesus grew to manhood, apprenticing with his earthly father. He earned His way as a carpenter.

On their pilgrimage to Jerusalem in His twelfth year, Mary became quite frantic when He stayed behind in the temple, but Dodi remained with Him and watched over him.

If only she knew.

The tribute of his constant care never bored him or caused him angst. His dear charge proved no difficulty in those formative years . . . he could have easily handled the duty alone.

Then he reached thirty years of age.

From a quiet life in the background, all changed.

No wonder God had given him a full legion of the host to protect His Son.

Three and one-half years of earth's days passed with Jesus proclaiming the coming of God's Kingdom.

The Master confirmed his words with signs, wonders, and miracles before the day Dodi heard clearly Words he never wanted to hear.

DO NOT OBSTRUCT THEM FROM TAKING MY SON TO THE CROSS

CHAPTER TWO

The lash came down swift and hard. Dodi flinched. He wanted to look away but could not. Thirty-three and one-half years before, he'd been charged to watch over the Creator's Anointed.

His dispatch had given him great joy through the years, but that was all in the past, not enough pleasure to compensate for what they did to his Lord.

Another strike.

The whip's leather tips entwined with bits of bone and metal dug deep.

How could He endure it?

One Word and Dodi would slay them all. Or he would whisk the Master away just as in Nazareth when they tried to push Him off the cliff—or in the Temple when they were going to stone Him.

Wings fluttered, and an awareness of an angel landing behind him. Dodi tore his eyes away from Jesus to glance over his shoulder. His old friend, looking like a freshly created angel of the host, nodded once.

He responded in like manner before looking back only to see the brute bring down the whip again.

"Lord God Almighty, have mercy on Your only begotten Son."

"He must not."

"How is it that you are here, Namrel? Has the watch changed with no announcement in my hearing? I was not called?"

"No, it remains the same. The Lord released me early."

Another horrific blow cut through muscle. Blood dripped and spattered the stone around the whipping post. The Master made no sound.

Why? Why would He suffer it?

Dodi studied his friend for one drop of the water-clock. "God's glory still lingers on you."

"Yes, He said I'd have need of it."

"When?"

"He did not say."

Another blow bit into the Master's back. Blood and pieces of torn flesh flew. Soldiers jeered and egged on the brute with the whip—to hit Him even harder.

"How can he stand it, friend?"

The old cherub grabbed Dodi's shoulder. His wing feathers fluffed then settled again.

"Just now, words the Lord spoke to His prophet Isaiah came to my remembrance. 'But He was wounded for our transgressions. He was bruised for our iniquities. The chastisement of our peace was upon Him, and with His stripes we are healed.' "

The Master's tormenter wiped his brow, grabbed himself a quick drink, then raised the whip again, paused his arm high over his head a moment, then brought it down again.

The man's companions cheered.

What astonishing cruelty. If only they knew Whom they whipped.

"His love must be great to endure this beating."

"Yes, Yadiyad."

"So, this is how Jesus will bring judgment and cast out the prince of this world?"

"Yes, it is." Namrel unfurled his wings, ever watching the beating His Master suffered. "Bless the Almighty."

"Enough." The chief among the soldiers pointed to the post where Jesus knelt, barely able to keep Himself upright. "Release him."

Another pagan Roman soldier came holding a purple robe. Two lifted Him to His feet while another heathen placed the robe over his bloody shoulders.

A third man carried a circle of woven thorns and crammed it ruthlessly onto the Master's head for a crown. They spat on Him and mocked Him, shouting, "Hail the King of the Jews!"

If only those men knew. Dodi's heart ached.

The barbs pierced the brow of Jesus, and Blood dripped from the wounds. Oh, Lord! Lord! It is so wrong. Could these evil men be worth the price?

Dodi searched Jesus' face, hoping for any sign that he was to liberate Him, but none came.

Namrel touched his arm. "He has set his face to endure exactly as the Almighty inspired Isaiah to prophesy."

The Romans knelt then jeered and mocked the Master—Who said not a word—then they took him back to Pilate. The governor met them in the hall, directing that Jesus be taken out to the judgment seat.

"How many legions do you command?"

Dodi tore his eyes off his charge to face his friend. "Mine and two more."

His gaze returned to God's Son, amazed at what he heard. Pontius Pilate, Roman prefect over Judea, gave the Jews a choice. He almost begged them to release Jesus, but His own people hated Him so much.

They shouted with loud voices and demanded a thief be freed instead of the Lord's Anointed.

"Why do you ask of the host? Has the Lord spoken to you?"

"No." He pointed overhead. "The enemy amasses."

At least five legions of Lucifer's angels circled overhead, singing their songs of death and wicked victory.

How could the Creator allow His Son to be thus beaten—or His chosen people to cry for His death?

The Word! Just give the Word, and Dodi would spring into action. If it would not be spoken, he wanted to close his eyes, flee, but he could not.

The Pharisees shouted back to the Judean governor. "If you let this man go, you are no friend of Caesar! Whoever makes himself a king is no friend of Caesar!"

"Why, Namrel? They despise the Romans."

"Crucify Him! Crucify Him!"

"I know, but they hate Jesus more. He threatens their political agenda to maintain power over their people."

Dodi looked heavenward. How far would God let the charade go? Jesus was His Own Beloved Son!

From the east, Michael and what had to be all the host of heaven not already stationed in Jerusalem flew above those following his fallen brother, but they sang no songs. Dodi faced his charge again.

Pilate had a bowl filled with water brought to him then washed his hands in it. "I am innocent of this just man's blood."

The Jews—as one man—cried out. "His Blood be on us and our children!"

"Oh, Namrel!" His hand went to his heart. "Why would they say such a thing, cursing their own offspring?"

The cherub shook his head with an expression of absolute sorrow on his face. "So much of what the Lord spoke makes sense. It's just as Isaiah said, their hearts have been made fat."

They stripped off the purple robe, leaving Jesus wrapped only in his undergarment then returned his own robe and led him away.

On the way out of the city, Jesus, obviously weak from his beating, had trouble bearing the weight of the cross. Dodi stepped forward, but his friend and mentor grabbed his arm.

"You must not interfere."

One of the Romans compelled a man of Cyrene, named Simon, to carry the Master's cross for him. They led him outside of the city to a mound called Golgotha, Hill of the Skull.

About the third hour, they nailed him to the cross and lifted Him up between two malefactors who were also being crucified on that horrible day.

One mocked the Master, challenging Him to save them all, but the other asked for mercy.

The Lord turned his gaze upon the latter. "This day, you will be with me in Paradise."

Darkness fell upon the earth at midday, the sixth hour, and the ground shook with a great noise. Dodi looked skyward.

The whole host of heaven, including his legion, had made themselves known and flew full wing, blocking the star's rays from the world.

"When did the archangel call my legions?"

The old cherub's wings spread high and wide. "I know not. I am witness to God's Lamb being slain. The Jews required it by the hands of these Roman barbarians."

Dodi, too, bore witness, desirous of looking away but compelled to note every detail of all that was done to God's Anointed.

About the ninth hour, Jesus proclaimed, "Eloi, Eloi, lama sabachthani?" At last, the Beloved Son called out to His Father. Surely, God would give the order to—

Then He spoke again. "I thirst."

The Romans offered him vinegar with hyssop on a sponge.

Jesus accepted it then said, "It is finished." He bowed his head and gave up the ghost.

No order to stop the horror came from the Almighty.

In great sorrow, Dodi bowed his head.

How could it be?

Word from the Most High came to both angels, Namrel the first of the cherubs, and Dodi the last and most powerful of the host had finally been given leave to act.

Chapter Three

Flying to the foot of the cross in great haste, Dodi caught the Spirit of the Lord's Anointed as He fell from His dead body. The stench of sin emanating from his Master overwhelmed him.

How could it be that He Who never sinned was made sin? Dodi could not understand the horror. His orders gave him sway, but he would obey as the Almighty commanded.

Carry Jesus into Torment, he would.

Lucifer and his fallen angels—how could the brothers have chosen to follow him over their Creator? — shouted the victory. Their roar filled his ears.

"Oh, friend—"

"Remember, Yadiyad, they lie. Wait to see. God's plan still unfolds." Namrel touched his shoulder. "We must comply. He is God's Lamb."

Though Dodi didn't understand, never understood when Jesus spoke of His death with His disciples, he chose to take his friend's advice. But . . .

How could God's Son ever die?

Was He not the Alpha and Omega, the beginning and the end, immortal to everlasting? Yet, His flesh had perished. Dodi witnessed it, and he had his orders. He would carry The Master's Spirit to Torment.

"You are correct, as always. I know you are. I understand not why but will fulfill our duty."

Jesus spoke no words, neither moaned nor cried out in sobs.

Dodi and Namrel carried Him through the bowels of the world until reaching the outer edge of the earth's center then paused. He looked toward Paradise.

However beautiful there, however much he enjoyed visiting his friend there, that was not his destination. Oh, why had God condemned His Only Begotten Son to the fires of Torment?

The old cherub touched his wing to Dodi's. "It is written, He bore the sins of many. Our Lord became man. Scripture declares it is appointed for each man to die once. Now He, too, must face judgment as all men."

"But Torment?"

"Has He not been made sin?"

The flames' heat singed his feathers and his hair, but . . . What of Jesus?

Still, orders were orders. Dodi would never think of disobeying Almighty God. Setting his face like flint—exampled by the Lord on his way to Jerusalem for Passover, knowing full well the Jews sought His very life—he lowered dear Jesus to the surface of the boiling mass of lava.

On its surface, flames danced and flickered.

How could He stand it?

The closer Dodi flew, the louder the screams and moans of the sinful sounded.

"Please, help me!"

"Water! Water!"

"Stranger! Come and cool my tongue, please!"

The cries of the condemned sounded from near and far away. Once and again, the semblance of a hand or even a face would boil up, only to be pulled down beneath the roiling surface again.

Surely God's Son would not sink into it.

"Lord, have mercy."

The heat proved unbearable. Dodi hovered slightly above the surface, wondering how the Son could tolerate it.

Clawed hands reached out, grabbing for the Lord. Gnarly bald heads with gruesome faces sat above bony shoulders and cackled hideously.

"Give Him to us! See His sin? Look at the way it clings to the man! Boundless will be His punishment. Give Him over! Let Him fall! Release Him!"

Their screeches and jeers pierced Dodi's heart. How could he do it? How could he not? With so great a reluctance he could barely stand it, he lowered his Master to the surface of Hades.

As His holy feet neared the molten fire, a light shown from above. Jesus walked on the path of God's living Word.

Praise the Almighty! He did not sink into the lava as His tormentors wanted. Rather, He walked just above the molten rock, slowly forward, one foot ahead of the other.

"Father," He called, stepping further toward the center of the molten lake of fire, staying just above its flaming surface.

"Look!" The cherub, hovering as far overhead as possible, pointed in the direction the Master traversed.

There, standing at the far cliff, along the edge of Paradise stood dozens upon dozens of men and women who gazed intently at the Lord as He strode toward them.

More than Dodi had ever seen together at one time— a great mass of humanity.

"Who are they?"

Namrel laughed. "You surely see and recognize Adam and Eve. Their son Abel stands with them. To their far side," Namrel pointed to the left, "are the patriarchs of old. Seth! I see Enoch and Methuselah.

The prophet Daniel called them the watchers, the holy ones."

With one powerful flap, Dodi lifted himself up. "And the prophets are there! Behind them, Israel's kings who followed after God's Ways. All are from Paradise? Has it emptied?"

"I know not, but those of His Kingdom have long desired to see this day."

Giant shadows moving above pulled Dodi's attention upwards still. Two archangels circled overhead before coming to roost on opposites sides of the Lord floating above the brimstone.

"Where is Gabriel?"

"I know not where God's messenger is."

The Lord continued on the Word's path until He stood at the edge of the brimstone lake, facing the throng.

"What exactly is happening here, Namrel?"

"It is written that the judges may judge them. That they shall justify the righteous and condemn the wicked. So these are to judge, but God Himself is the final judge."

"I see. I think."

"Guilty!" The accuser Lucifer pointed at Jesus. "You broke the Law!"

The great and beloved archangel Michael rose a few feet in the air then settled back, folding his wings. "Wrong, my brother! This man is entirely and completely innocent."

The first man created in God's own image stepped forward. "We will hear the evidence." Adam gazed toward the biggest, grandest, most beautiful angel ever created. "Lucifer, present your case."

Chapter Four

Dodi flew closer to his charge Who continued to remain silent. For the longest, the fallen archangel surveyed the crowd of judges before turning his gaze on Jesus.

"You broke God's law! You worked on the Sabbath!" He turned back toward Adam. "He encouraged His disciples to do work on the Sabbath. He should have been stoned many times, but . . ."

He whirled and pointed directly at Dodi. "This angel of the host interfered! The Son of Mary is a sinner! He received His just reward on the cross! He must be condemned!"

Another flap of Michael's powerful wings landed him beside Jesus, facing his youngest brother. "No, Lucifer! He did not break the Sabbath nor cause His disciples to do so."

God's highest warrior angel beckoned toward the great crowd of witnesses. "Moses! Come forward."

The man to whom the great I AM gave the law eased through the others to stand shoulder to shoulder with Adam.

"Tell us about the Sabbath."

The great man to Whom the Lord appeared at the burning bush on Mount Sinai stepped forward, in front of the first man.

"I AM instructed me to tell the children of Israel to remember the Seventh Day and keep it holy. From the evening star of Day Six until the same of the Sabbath, His people were to rest and do no work."

"Is that it? No work?"

"No. Specifically, they could kindle no fire. Preparations were to be made on the Sixth Day for the Seventh, the Sabbath."

"Anything else?"

"Yes, there is. The seventh year is also a Sabbath in which one cannot sow their fields or prune their vineyards."

The archangel bowed his head slightly toward the man whom God had hidden in the cleft of the rock when He passed by. "Thank you."

Returning the gesture in like manner, Moses stepped back next to Adam.

"Dodi." Michael faced him. "Since the birth of His beloved Son, the Almighty charged you to watch over Him. Have you ever left His side?"

"No."

"Has Jesus worked on the Sabbath? Has He kindled a fire or sowed a field or pruned His vineyard in the seventh year?"

"No, Michael. He has not."

With loud blasts of his horns, and the rolling of the harps beneath his wings, Lucifer rose into the air. "Liar! He healed on the Sabbath! He allowed His followers to reap corn on the Sabbath! He is a sinner!"

Looking again to the giver of God's Law, Michael shook his head. "Moses! Is healing work?"

"Not if He only spoke the Words. You see, the Jewish scribes and teachers have perverted what I AM commanded me to write."

"Please give us an example."

"Three times, upon His command, I wrote, 'Do not seethe a kid in its mother's milk.' They have taken that to mean that meat and dairy may not be together in the same container. They err."

"Could they have misunderstood God's meaning?"

"I've found the I AM means exactly what He says. The Almighty's instruction is plain, made simple for man's benefit—he should not cook, boil, or simmer a kid in its mother's milk."

"I see."

"How could He be any clearer? Men add false teaching from their intellect."

"What about traveling on the Sabbath? How far may one walk?"

"I AM made no pronouncement regarding the length of travel. He wanted His people to remember Him on the Seventh Day and rest, not be under so many burdensome rules."

"What of His disciples reaping on the Sabbath? Is that not work?"

"They hungered. By law, an Israelite may pluck ears of standing corn from a brother's field if he only uses his hands."

Michael whirled around. "Dodi, did they use anything other than their hands?"

"No."

"What else, Brother?"

Dodi loved Michael's expression as he turned and faced Lucifer once more.

"The way I see it, Jesus never violated the Sabbath and certainly never instructed His disciples to do so."

CHAPTER FIVE

"That is not for you to decide, Brother! You are not a judge!"

The disdain in the archangel's voice troubled Dodi, but Michael was right. Jesus never violated the Sabbath. Not once.

Why, He lived a perfect life the whole time His feet walked on earth! He'd only done good—never any evil as accused. Yet, on the cross, He became sin, carrying all the sins of the world.

Lucifer pointed at Jesus with a wing tip.

"He dishonored his father and mother! He should have been taken out and stoned when He was but a boy, only twelve years of age. Remember? He stayed in Jerusalem without their permission or knowledge!"

"Wrong!" Dodi couldn't help himself. "The Great I AM Who is His Father compelled Him to go to the Temple."

The devil-incarnate glared.

Michael stepped in front of his brother, facing Dodi. "You heard the Creator send Him?"

"Yes, I did. Even at such a tender age, His zeal for God's house proved to take over His heart."

"What happened once Mary and Joseph found Him there?"

"He immediately went with them back to Nazareth and remained in submission to His parents, as always."

"So, He honored both his Heavenly Father and his earthly parents?"

"Yes, He did. To the jot and tittle."

Michael spun around. "What else, Brother?"

"What else? What else? I can see how this farce is going! Excuses! For everything, excuses! Jesus of Nazareth ate numerous times without washing His hands! What can you say about that? I can't wait to hear your excuses!"

The archangel looked to Moses. "Sir, did God ever tell you to wash with water before eating?"

"No, He did not. Not at all. That's only another tradition of the Pharisees and scribes. The Almighty gave no such commandant."

"He touched the dead! And a woman with an issue of blood! He didn't wash his hands or clothes after either!"

A small snicker escaped from Dodi.

With one mighty flap, Lucifer rose four feet into the air. "What do you find humorous about that, Centurion?"

"My name is Dodi, as I am I AM's beloved." He held up four fingers.

"The woman touched the hem of his garment and by her faith, she was healed. He never touched her. Lazarus . . . He called out from the tomb, telling him only to come forth. The young maid? Yes. He took her hand, but she was alive before He touched her, as was the mother's only son."

One by one, he folded his fingers back. "There is, nor has there ever been, any sin this man has committed."

"He traveled with prostitutes and ate with sinners!"

Facing the throng of judges, Michael called out the prophet Isaiah. "Sir, please tell us what God inspired you to write about the meek and the brokenhearted."

The old prophet stepped forward and stood beside Moses.

"The Spirit of the Lord God came upon me. He anointed me to preach good tidings unto the meek. He sent me to bind up the brokenhearted, to proclaim liberty to the captives, and to open the prison doors for those who were bound."

"Did you speak of yourself or another?"

"I spoke of Him." Isaiah pointed to Jesus. "Not of myself, but God's only begotten Son."

"How else was He to fulfill the prophecy than to be kind and accepting of those God sent Him?"

Michael turned from Satan to the throng. "Have you heard enough?"

Adam nodded, then faced the others, raising both hands into the air. "What say ye? Is there any sin found in this man?"

Thunderous shouts of 'No!' and 'Never!' pleased Dodi to the depths of his being.

Praise be to the Almighty, the Creator of the Universe Who is worthy to receive all the glory, honor, and praise! Just as he knew it should be!

Lucifer cursed, flapped his powerful wings, and rose off the molten lake.

The Lord held out his hand. "The keys."

"No! Never!"

The fallen angels echoed their leader's words then extolled Lucifer's great beauty and power.

Legions of the hosts who remained loyal to the Creator flew overhead and answered in praise and worship songs honoring the One and only true God. Everything in Dodi wanted to join them, to add his harmony to their melodies, but he refrained and stayed with the Master as charged.

One flew from the gathering of the hosts and bowed low toward the Lord. He sang in a crystal-clear baritone. Three more joined him, echoing a tenor harmony.

"Lion of the Tribe of Judah! The bright and Morning Star. The Rose of Sharon. King of Kings! Lord of

Lords! By righteousness, You have conquered death and hell and will live forever more!"

"They sing the truth, Lucifer." He did not withdraw His hand. "The keys."

"No! You are nothing more than a usurper! Born in sin! These fools are blinded!"

THIS IS MY BELOVED SON IN WHOM I AM WELL PLEASED

The archangel snarled, looked heavenward, then scowled.

HEAR YE HIM

He extended the keys to death and hell over Jesus' palm and dropped them. The Lord caught them midair. The fallen one disappeared into the clouds above within a blink.

A shadow fell on the throng as Gabriel circled once overhead then landed. The archangel handed Dodi a fine robe then encircled the Lord with his wings.

"Take off those filthy garments, Master. Clothe Him as fits the King of Kings!"

Namrel joined him. "Here, put this on his head." The old cherub knelt before the Lord. Dodi did likewise, and the archangel placed the golden crown on His scarred head.

The Master held his hand toward the pit. It opened, exposing all those poor souls therein. With a loud voice the Lord spoke to the damned.

"Repent, you workers of iniquity. Renounce your idolatry and come unto Me and my Father. I am the One and only Way to Him. On the earth, you served the father of lies. I am the Truth."

His eyes searched the hearts of the evil congregation. "There are no lies in Me. You have a choice, deny yourself and all those false gods you worshipped, and follow Me for everlasting Life."

Thousands upon thousands clamored over each other, scrambling from the pit, climbing onto the backs of those who hesitated. They wept and accepted the Lord's forgiveness.

"Thank You, Messiah!"

"Bless You, Savior!"

The Master spoke again. "They who shall be accounted worthy to obtain the world and the resurrection from the dead neither marry, nor are given in marriage. Neither can they die any more.

"You are equal unto the angels and have this opportunity to become children of God again, being the children of the resurrection.

"Come unto me all ye that labor and are heavy laden, and I will give you rest."

Thousands more made their way from the pit, but not all. A crowd hung back together, shouting curses and blasphemies.

It shocked Dodi that more did not. "Why would so many still reject Him?"

"Pride." Namrel spoke in his hearing. "Their arrogance has blinded them . . . Plus, they have believed the lies so long, it has become truth to them."

From the pit, men shouted over each other.

"You're only a man! Not a god!"

"You broke the laws!"

"You're nothing but a cheating liar!"

"You aren't any Christ, and You didn't save anyone!"

How could He remain so calm?

"I told you plainly, and you refused to believe—even though the works that I do in my Father's name bear witness of me. You do not believe for you are not of My sheep."

Momentarily, He bowed His head.

"As I said unto you, My sheep hear My voice. I know them, and they follow Me. I give them eternal life and they will never perish. No man may pluck them from My hand either, for my Father gave them to Me, and He is greater than all. My Father and I are One."

"Liar!"

Dodi's heart hurt for the non-believers, but they had an opportunity to choose the Master . . . His head bowed in sorrow and disbelief, but the Master loved and held a few more of those from Hades.

Chapter Six

As soon as the last to accept the Lord's forgiveness and salvation and was carried to Paradise, Dodi bowed to his Master.

"With Your approval, Lord, we will carry You now to Paradise."

"Yes." The Lord held out his arms. Dodi flew into position beneath one, and Namrel, the other.

Slowly they rose as songs of praise and worship sounded both from the watchers in Paradise and from the host of angels in the heavenlies.

Across the guff that separated Torment from Paradise, Dodi and Namrel carried Him. The great crowd parted, forming a corridor. Adam and Seth at its head, the patriarchs, prophets, and kings in line behind them.

Dodi and Namrel lowered the Master.

The first man, his wife, and sons went to one knee.

"Jesus! Son of David! You are the King of Kings and the Lord of Lords! There is no one like unto You!"

The host flew overhead adding, "Holy! Holy! Holy is the Lord!" Their voices extolled the excellence and majesty of the Son of God. Dodi loved it and joined in the chorus. He loved the Lord!

What a turnaround!

God so loved the world that He gave His only begotten Son as ransom for many—for all who would believe and receive.

The great Creator even sent Him to hell's fire so that those who accepted His sacrifice would not have to suffer torment.

What a mighty God he served!

Hanging back as the Lord walked amongst the captives of Paradise, Dodi looked to his old friend. "What now? Do you know?"

"Only that, for now, He is to remain here. There are so many who need to hear the Good News. They must decide."

"Decide? Decide what?"

"Whether they will accept Him."

"Namrel! You surely jest, my friend! Who in their right mind would reject Him now?"

"You would think thus, would you not? But do you remember when He said on earth that He was the Way? How no man could go to the Father except by Him?"

"I do, of course."

"Since their creation, man has had a choice. He always has a choice—to accept or reject God's beloved and precious Way."

"Jesus."

"Yes, Yadiyad. Before the shedding of His blood, His sacrifice on the cross, there was no remission of their sin available. In their fallen state, men could not enter into the presence of the Most High God, but now . . ."

"Now the Messiah has made a Way. His work is finished."

"Yes, and now comes the joy set before Him. He will share, and men and women throughout Paradise must choose."

Searching the crowds following his charge, Dodi recognized the thief on the cross who hung adjacent to the Master. His heart was made glad to see the man run to the Lord that first day in Paradise.

He hugged Him, patting His back over and again, pure joy on his face. Without seeing it, Dodi knew the sun's light faded over Jerusalem, and the night passed.

Teaching and sharing the Good News continued in Paradise as the second day from the cross dawned. What would the disciples be doing?

Would the Sadducees and Pharisees be celebrating? Or had they realized their grave mistake?

While Dodi and his kind needed no rest, men on the edge still did. Those new to Paradise stirred to the Master's teachings.

His dear friend pointed a wingtip toward the Son as over a thousand people approached. "See how they come to Him and believe? At least until the morning of the first day of the new week."

"What happens then?"

"His Spirit will return to his body."

"You know this, how?"

Namrel put a finger to his lips. "I will explain later. Let us hear the Lord's words."

Drawing near to the edge of the crowd gathered around Jesus, Dodi listened. The Lord preached the Good News—all about how He left His throne in Heaven and came to earth born of Holy Spirit.

Oh, how he loved the Master's story! After all, he'd practically lived it with Him! Well, the end had been hard, very hard indeed.

All those He adored and died for accepted His gift of salvation. They encircled their Savior, singing His praises. Dodi stood with his friend Namrel on the outskirts of the Lord's new disciples.

A man left the throng and approached him.

The cherub hugged the fellow then looked to Dodi. "Do you remember Abel?"

"Of course. Hello, son of Adam. It is a pleasure to see you here."

"And it is wonderful to see you again. How have you faired these many years, Centurion?"

"He chose a name finally. He decided on Dodi."

"Beloved, I like that. It's very appropriate. The love of the Lord has so impacted me! Now I will spend eternity in Heaven with my Creator—all because of His Son and what He's sacrificed for me."

Then the Master Himself stepped over toward Abel. Dodi looked intently to see if there might be any service he could perform, but Jesus only smiled. He faced Abel.

"You should share with these of the time you met the first of the cherubim."

"Gladly, Lord."

"It happened on the occasion of the thirtieth anniversary of Meve birthing my brother Cain and myself—the first time Padam invited us to join him going to the high place. We were to make our first offering to the Creator."

"How exciting it must have been for you."

Namrel bumped Dodi's shoulder with his own, as though perhaps the cherub was telling him not to interrupt the story, but the angel of the host wasn't on the surface anymore, but in the bowels of the earth.

After a star's twinkle he decided perhaps his friend was right.

"Indeed, but my brother's grains… Abba rejected. Though the cloud of His presence vanished, the Lord's golden afterglow proved a wondrous experience. His glory proved so bright I could hardly bear it and covered my face. After a fistful of heartbeats, I peeked between my fingers. Cain was nowhere to be seen."

Tempted as Dodi was to ask if his brother had left with his father, he didn't want to interrupt the man's story or get another bump from Namrel.

Then as if Able had heard his thoughts, he answered. "Padam remained prostrate beside me before the center altar."

"Where then was your brother?" Had he said that out loud or just thought it? No one had looked at him. All eyes remained on Adam's second son.

"I knew not where my brother had gone. When God had rebuked my brother, I remained perfectly still. I dared not look or add to his shame. Pushing myself up, I glanced toward the path, but he was gone."

So many questions Dodi wanted to ask. He'd never heard the story before.

"I could not see him or even hear his footfalls before an eagle screamed overhead. It dove straight at me. At the last blink, the mighty bird veered and soared on the wind's current over the valley below."

"What did you do?"

"I grabbed my shawl and prayer blanket then quietly backed away from the sacred place, following its flight."

"Did your father join you?" Dodi covered his mouth with his off wingtip, but again no one looked his way, but Abel. Had the man heard his question?

"I looked back just before losing sight of the high place, but Padam remained prostrate and motionless. He wasn't going after Cain. A tear rolled down my cheek."

"I'm sad for you, hearing of your plight."

"Everything would have been so wonderful if only my headstrong brother had sacrificed a lamb. My heart hurt for him. Even after all the fights and harsh words spoken, I loved my brother."

"That is true, Abel." The Master embraced the young man. "Your heart was always filled with love."

"And even more with my present understanding of the sin offerings. If only I could have helped Cain comprehend. Father God told him if he would do what was right, he would be accepted."

"As all may."

"Yes. Anyway, I continued along the path, still hearing Padam's glorious praises. My hope was to catch my brother while there might be time enough still."

"Once past Guard Rock, I broke into a run going down the mountain after my twin. I found him on the path, leaning against the tree we'd named Last Look years prior. I urged him to come back."

A change came over Abel, as though he had been transported back to that time and place. He told his story as if truly speaking to Cain.

" 'Come, Brother. If we hurry, you can still make an offering.' I so wanted to encourage him.

" 'Forget it. Our father's God rejected me. He is not my god!'

"His words were incredulous to my ears. 'Don't be a snake-in-the-tree! The Lord hasn't rejected you! Only your offering! He wants you to do what is right.'"

"I grabbed my brother's arm. 'Hurry. We can still choose a yearling and be back to the high place before long shadows.'

"Cain's eyes blazed." Abel looked to Dodi then Namrel with a great sorrow. "He balled his fist. I braced myself, but the blow never came. The fire in my twin's eyes cooled to a cold stare before he patted my shoulder. In those silent moments, a concern for my mother and sister gripped me . . . as if their hearts suffered some unknown great pain. It was quite strange.

"I couldn't imagine why that would be, but my brother's voice brought me back from my musings.

"He said, 'Yes, you may be right. It's worth a try. Let's go fetch a yearling.' He nodded with an odd smile and added, 'But hurry. There's something I must show you first.'

"He spun around and trotted toward his furthest field. I ran after him and begged him to let whatever it was to wait. My lambs were in the opposite direction, and he needed one to make a blood sacrifice and be accepted, but he didn't stop until he reached the field's edge.

" 'This won't take long,' he promised then pointed toward a spot not fifty strides away. 'See? It's there.'

"Nothing worth any delay came to my view. I followed though, asking him what could be so important. Then Cain knelt, picked something up, and swung around toward me.

"The fire returned to his eyes. With it, an evil I'd never seen before. My brother's words escaped through clenched teeth, though his volume could barely be heard over the screaming eagle overhead.

" 'Never again will you take my place.' It confused me, so I inquired what he meant. Suddenly my brother roared, 'I am the firstborn!'

"Of course, you are. I know that. I held out both hands, palms up, and asked, 'Why do you think that? When have I ever tried to take your place, Brother? What have I done?'

"He only screamed that he hated me. He lowered his shoulder and charged. At first, I balled my own fists then consciously relaxed them."

"Should you not have defended yourself?" Dodi scratched his forehead. "I don't understand the ways of men." The Master smiled at him. Had he said that aloud, or . . . Well, He was Omnipotent after all.

"I would not, could not, fight my brother again. The Lord's peace carried from the high place still enveloped me, though I must admit confusion warred against it.

"It was strange. With each step, it seemed Cain ran slower and slower. A crazed expression twisted and contorted his face. He raised the rock in his hand above his head as he advanced, but it made no matter.

"I determined not to defend myself. I tried to reason with him, reminding him of what God said—that he must master—

"That's when the impact slammed me to the ground, forcing the breath from my lungs. My brother's weight impeded another. Though Cain held the stone above his head, God's peace still permeated my soul."

"No! Your own brother?"

"Yes. I looked into his eyes and wasn't able to imagine how there could be so much hate and anger there. The rock crashed down. Pain exploded in my head and then vanished as quickly.

"My eyes lost focus. Blackness engulfed me.

"I closed my eyes as if to sleep and experienced a sensation of great speed carrying me toward a bright light. Consciousness returned, and a brilliant golden glow encompassed me. I floated peacefully downward.

"I had no idea where the pain had gone. I traced my fingertips over my head. No blood. Neither any wound. Understanding proved so difficult. I called to my brother.

"Cain? Where are you? Put the rock down. We must hurry and choose a lamb. Those words formed in my mind, and I spoke them, but where the sound of it went, I didn't know."

Dodi understood that perfectly!

"The light dimmed as strong arms wrapped around me then set my feet onto firm ground again. I stood in the midst of a meadow, a place I had never seen, but recognized from my parents' stories.

"I thought it had to be Eden. Released, I turned and faced a winged being." Abel chuckled. "I thought him to be an odd-looking man at first. He stood half-a-head shorter than me."

The man held out his flattened hand over Namrel's head, grinning.

"The being wore a long white robe with a band of golden cloth across his chest. I asked him, 'Who are you?' But again, no audible words came forth—though he did respond.

" 'I am called Namrel.' His smile seemed understanding over my confusion of speaking without benefit of sound, how it puzzled me. That's how I met my friend. I asked endless questions at first, but he remained so patient with me.

"My first was if that was my parents' Garden of Eden. The birdman chuckled and shook his head telling me, 'No, my new friend. You are in Paradise.'

Just then, Jesus stepped aside. Dodi could not believe the resemblance. Another man had joined him and the group who could only be Abel's twin, Cain. The brothers looked at each for a heartbeat then raced to embrace.

Abel leaned back. "I was hoping against hope! Bless God that you accepted His grace and love, dear Brother."

"Yes, will you forgive me, Abel?"

"Of course."

Cain held his hand out, and a woman joined the brothers.

"Sheria!"

"Sister!"

All three hugged and laughed together, then the first man and his wife emerged from the crowd. Dodi recognized them straightaway.

"Padam!"

"Meve! Dear mother! It's so wonderful to see you both again!"

Adam and Eve embraced their children, and Dodi smiled, his heart filled with love and admiration for the chosen of the Lord.

The Master laughed, obviously enjoying the jubilant reunion. He stood and turned to the watching crowd.

"Blessed are the poor in spirit: for theirs is the kingdom of heaven. Blessed are they that mourn: for they shall be comforted. Blessed are the meek: for they shall inherit the earth.

"Blessed are they which do hunger and thirst after righteousness: for they shall be filled. Blessed are the merciful: for they shall obtain mercy and blessed are the pure in heart: for they shall see God.

"Also blessed are the peacemakers: for they shall be called the children of God."

"Thank You, Messiah!"

"I'm so glad you have chosen to accept my gift of salvation for I Am the Way, the Truth, and the Life, and no man may come to the Father but by Me."

While the first family sang praise and worship songs, extolling the goodness of the Master, He strolled away and continued preaching the Good News.

He spoke until all those within hearing bowed their knee, confessed Him as their Lord, and accepted His great sacrifice to be able to join the Father.

Dodi had seen it so many times before on earth, but it never got old or tiresome. Jesus ended by laying hands on His new disciples. He walked on deeper into Paradise, the place for the righteous, created to resemble Eden.

What could he do but follow the Lord? Namrel, too, left the joyful family and followed the Master with him. Dodi leaned in close.

"Tell me. How is it that you know the Lord will return to his body on the third day? Must He?"

"Yes, my friend. How many times did Jesus say, 'Tear down this temple, and I will rebuild it in three days'?"

"Many, too many to count. That was one thing they mocked Him for when He hung on that cursed tree. But what has that to do with my question? I do not understand. What does it mean, Namrel?"

"Well, the temple He referred to was His body—the Temple of God, and He inspired David to write the scripture, Therefore my heart is glad, and my glory rejoices! My flesh also shall rest in hope. For You will not leave my soul in hell, neither will You suffer Your Holy One to see corruption. Do you see now, dear Yadiyad?"

"I do not."

"God will quicken His mortal body—His flesh which died on the cross—and His Spirit will return to it. There can be no other way."

As soon as he caught the concept, Dodi's heart swelled. What a sight to see! But then Jesus had called Lazarus forth from the dead.

He nodded toward where the Master had stopped to talk with more residents of Paradise; He loved the truth of Him being the bread. Dodi could imagine the food of men.

"Come. Let us join the crowd. See if there are any who do not accept the Lord."

"How could they not? These men were righteous when they lived on earth since they're in Paradise. Isn't that accurate?"

"It is, but their righteousness is as filthy rags in the sight of our holy God. So as all men, they need the Blood that Jesus shed to wash them white as snow."

"I am the Bread of Life. He who comes to Me will never hunger, and he who believes on Me will never thirst. I've told you. You have seen Me yet chose not to believe.

"All those the Father gives me will come to me and never be cast out. I came from Heaven not to do My Own will but the will of Him Who sent Me. My Father's will is for all who sees the Son and believes on Him to have everlasting life.

"I will raise them up on the last day."

Oh, the glory of the Lord!

How could it be that men would ever reject Him, Dodi could not comprehend.

On the edge, night fell on Jerusalem in the second day since His crucifixion. The evil ones reveled and caroused in their wickedness, serving the snake, singing his praise and worshipping him.

The men even offered the lives of their children to false gods!

How could they have come so low?

Chapter Seven

Paradise was awash with angels of the host. Dodi watched until all its inhabitants, save the few souls still speaking with the Lord, were lifted by his brothers and carried up through the portal.

Soon they would be in Heaven. He himself longed to return, but not until he and Namrel went with the Master.

The Creator returned to the meadow and bid him to sit next to Him—a place not accustomed to Dodi—but there in Paradise, he could relax a bit—nothing to be on watch for.

Those who killed the Lord remained on the surface, thinking they had won a great victory. In only a few more hours as they counted time, all would change.

Weeping and mourning would be turned to joy beyond measure, and the men's smugness to consternation, worry, and disbelief.

"Abel, there's something I would like you to see." His Lord placed His hand on the man's knee. "Everyone open your minds' eyes."

Dodi did as the others.

The sun rose in the east, as every other morning for the forty-five years since Eve's creation. That day, however, proved like only one other.

An overwhelming sorrow filled her being as she thought of it. She had caused the banishment from Eden, and the blame weighed on her shoulders—all her blame because of disobedience and manipulations.

That morning, beside the lifeless, cold body of her dear Abel laying on the ground weighed even more heavily on her—both her flesh and her heart.

How could all her children be lost to her?

The overwhelming grief . . . How could she stand the pain yet live?

Adam threw out another shovel full of dirt. While she watched her husband dig the grave that would receive her second son, the unanswered questions reverberated through her soul.

No soothing balm presented itself though, nothing to help her, comfort her, and give her peace. More dirt flew from the knee-deep hole, and the fresh mound beside it grew, just as the weight in her gut.

Her life had come to ruin again just like in Eden. But why? What had she done?

"Tell me why, Husband. Why would God be so cruel? What have I done to deserve such sorrow?"

Adam continued digging without comment.

The nagging questions tormented her. She lowered herself to the grass, still wet with dew that rose each even to water the earth.

"Will you answer?"

"This was not Abba's doing." He faced her. "Better to ask why Cain killed his brother."

"But . . . surely there he carried no intent in the act. It had to be . . . only an accident. Cain even said so himself before he left."

Though Adam shared his version of the first murder in the land of the living, she preferred to believe her firstborn's.

"No, my precious. There was no fighting." He shook his head. "Examine your son's shell. Do you see any marks? Or bruises? No, because there are none. Only the one blow that opened his head. The wound was deliberate, intentional."

With all the tears Eve cried during the long night, how could more well up for her soul? She bowed her head and closed her wet eyes.

"Even if you are right, God allowed it. He had to have permitted it, didn't He? So then . . . why did Abba not only allow Abel's life with us to end, but banish my living son?"

"I know not."

"I am the mother of all the living, you said!" Her voice rose to a screaming volume, sounding frantic and crazy even to her, but she cared not. "Where are my children? Tell me where my many beloved children are!"

Adam leaned on the shovel and shrugged.

"Why does He do anything, Eve? I know not Abba's mind, only His heart. I know He cares and loves us beyond measure. Yes, He is all powerful, but He gave us free wills, hoping we would choose His Way. When we do not, we suffer consequences—for example . . . having to leave Eden."

"I know. I'm sorry. I have repented."

"Our departure from our garden is not all your fault. You were deceived. I should have been there. Things will be right again though for our Creator loves us, wife. For our life, that is more than enough."

"But how can anything ever be right again? My babies!" She released a sob before continuing. "They are all gone! And you . . . refuse me others."

"We will wait upon the Lord, as we should have in the beginning."

Wrapping her arms across her bosom, she held in the profound grief, misery, and angst. Eve rocked, studying her beautiful son's face. It would surely be the death of her own flesh—she'd never hurt more.

How could it be possible to suffer any greater loss?

"I have seen forty-five summers, and you sixty. Truly, Husband, how long must we wait?" She spat the words.

"Until Abba gives His blessing, we will wait, Wife. I will not disobey God again, however long that may take." He stared at her for a few heartbeats then returned to digging.

"Have you . . . asked Him since . . .?"

Once more, he stopped his labor. "Yes, I have asked, and He said, 'Wait.' "

"Oh, husband, how can we bear it?" She leaned closer over her son's cold chest. "Please! Ask Him again!"

Then the scene playing out before Dodi's mind's eye suddenly moved to Paradise—close to where he sat with the others, and Abel cautiously stood. He obviously tried not to disturb the great lion, but the animal raised his head.

"Sleep on, my friend." The first words spoken aloud since the man had arrived in Paradise, words he heard with his ears, almost startled him.

As if the beast understood, he laid his head back and closed his eyes.

"If only Padam could know you lived here in Paradise with me."

After staring across the great divide a few heartbeats, Abel walked away. Easily enough, he found the home meadow and the rock house. With words of his mind, he called as he entered, "Namrel? Are you here?"

"Ah, you have returned." The familiar voice led him through his new home though no sound brushed either ear.

He strolled through the main room then past his resting nook. A deep-throated hum that he could actually hear spurred him along.

Upon reaching the last room on the east end, he stopped in his tracks. A giant angel looked over Namrel's folded wings as the cherub traced his finger over a page of his book.

Six breaths later, though Abel no longer needed to breathe, Namrel looked up, but the giant continued to stare intently at the cherub's odd markings.

"Hello, Abel. How was your nap?"

"Good, refreshing."

The giant lifted his head and spoke without words in Namrel's manner. "Forgive this angel's intrusion, young man, but your mother—"

"My mother? What about my mother? Is Meve here?"

The cherub held his hands up, palms facing Abel. "No, she remains on the edge. However, the pain—from your demise—has brought her low."

"I am sorry for dear Meve, but for some reason I know not, my sorrow fails to hurt my heart as it would in my father's valley."

"How could you be sad in the presence of God's joy? And besides, the Creator sent Centurion here with his one hundred to sing a ring of protection around her. This angel is one of the host we spoke of before."

"Did you say sing?" Abel stepped into the room. "Protection? From what does my mother need protection?"

Centurion looked toward Namrel, who spoke without sound. "Lucifer and his minions. They have deceived her twice before. Hopefully, her redemption draws nigh."

"And who's Lucifer?"

"The snake."

Realization dawned in Abel. He looked to the giant. "If Meve's in danger, I'll go with you. Why are you still here anyway?"

The giant nodded toward the book he studied. "My quiver was empty, but now it is full."

Abel backed a step from the doorway. "Then let's be gone."

Namrel stood. "Not possible."

"Why not?"

Centurion stepped toward Abel. "Come and see."

Outside, the giant angel lifted his head, spread his wings. Their magnificent height and breadth startled Abel. The angel of the host sang three crisp, clear notes.

After a pause, he whistled two more, and little bolts of blue light cut a circle in the expanse a furlough overhead.

One pull of Centurion's mighty wings shot him high into the air. He glanced once beneath his raised wing before disappearing through the blue hole.

Beside the Lord, Dodi opened his eyes and chuckled. "I remember that day vividly. It was awesome." He looked at Abel. "Do you remember what you asked Namrel when I flew away?"

"Of course. I wanted to know what you had filled your quiver with."

"Yes. When I sang all the new songs of praise, my melodies for the battle, I plucked so many feathers that day. And only lost a few. Victory in war is always sweet."

For a star's twinkle, Dodi pondered. Surely others had commented on it, but he had to ask the man. "Has anyone told you how much you resemble God?"

"Yes, most every angel of the host!" He chuckled. "I have met many since Namrel introduced me to you. I believe most every one of your brothers has mentioned it."

The first cherub laughed. "Shortly, you will see for yourself." Namrel turned his attention to the Master. "One of Dodi's thousand has returned to take these to Heaven, and if You are ready, Lord, it is time to go."

CHAPTER EIGHT

Dodi cared little over being in the Lord's dank tomb, but orders were orders. Never would he disobey the Master. He folded his wings in tight, then bumped his shoulder to Namrel's.

"The women come."

"I see them. It's almost time to show ourselves."

Though Dodi knew his part well, he submitted to his dear old mentor and friend and honored him with the last word. The cherub spoke to the ladies who sought the Master.

"Why seek you the living among the dead? He is not here, but is risen: remember how He spoke to you when yet in Galilee?

"He told you then that the Son of Man must be delivered into the hands of sinful men, be crucified, and that on the third day, how He would rise again."

Astonishment and disbelief etched their faces. In great haste and without further comment, they departed.

Were they afraid of dear Namrel? Or himself?

"We need to hurry and catch up with the Master."

"Yes." Dodi led the way, flying to where the Messiah walked toward a village called Emmaus. He joined two of His disciples, but . . . they did not recognize Him. How could it be?

Remaining behind the Master as He conversed with the men, Dodi remained unseen, listening, and love swelled his heart.

The Master expounded on the Scriptures—how all that had been written of Him must be completed. Once inside and after bread had been broken, the men's eyes were finally opened, and they rejoiced with their Savior.

Jesus glanced at Dodi and smiled. He wrapped his wings around the One he so loved and whisked Him away. The master waited until those two disciples returned to Jerusalem and joined their brothers.

"The Lord is alive!"

"What?"

"How could it be?"

"We saw them lower Him and take His body from the cross!"

Extending his wings, Dodi revealed Jesus Himself, standing in their midst.

"Peace be unto you."

Why would His own be terrified? What possessed the foolish men? Did they suppose their Messiah to be a ghost?

"Why are ye troubled? And why do thoughts arise in your hearts? Behold, My hands and My feet. See? It is I, Myself. Handle me and see. A spirit has not flesh and bones, as ye see I do."

The Master held out his hands and his feet for their examination. "Have ye any meat?"

"Yes, Lord!" One gave him a piece of broiled fish, and another offered a honeycomb. He took it and ate the food before them.

"These are the Words I spoke unto you, while I was yet with you, men. All things must be fulfilled which were written in the law of Moses, in the books of the prophets, and in the Psalms concerning Me."

He promptly opened their understanding so that they might comprehend the Scriptures.

"It is written, and thus it behooved Christ to suffer then rise from the dead on the third day so that repentance and remission of sins should be preached in My name among all nations, beginning at Jerusalem. Ye are My witnesses of these things."

Into His eleven, He poured His love and teachings while He still walked on the earth. He had many encounters with them—but never non-believers—for forty days before the fullness of time came.

On that very special day, Dodi's closest few from his chief cohort and Namrel stood with him on the Mount of Olives, concealed from those Jesus had invited to witness His homegoing.

"Lord, will You restore again the Kingdom of Israel?"

"It is not for you to know the times or the seasons which the Father has planned, but ye shall receive power when the Holy Ghost comes upon you, and ye shall be my witnesses in Jerusalem and all of Judaea. Also, in Samaria and even to the uttermost parts of the earth."

The Master nodded to Dodi who turned and commanded his cohort to take the Lord home.

With reverence and bowed heads, the angels of the host engulfed the King of Kings and lifted Him heavenward. Dodi and Namrel revealed themselves to the Lord's disciples.

"Oh, men of Galilee! Why do you stand gazing up into heaven? This same Jesus which is taken up from you into heaven shall come again in a like manner as you have seen Him go today."

Dodi spread his wings, grabbed Namrel's hand, then flew to his cohort. The cherub took his place at the Master's right hand while Dodi flew ahead and whistled the portal open.

He charged the rest of his legion to close ranks around the Lord. Using the song Gabriel gave him, he flew the lead, straight and true.

The heavenward portal opened over the Crystal Sea. Dodi landed six furlongs out of I AM's manifest presence. Those whom the Master had redeemed stood in mass.

John, Jesus's cousin, the one they called the Baptizer, stepped forward. "Behold, the Lamb of God! He who was dead but now is alive forevermore."

The son of Zachariah and Elizabeth knelt before the Lord of the Host, followed by all of Heaven's new inhabitants.

A rumble of praise and great happiness rose—a joyous noise such as Dodi had never heard since his creation. It blessed his ears then his heart, and he joined in crying, "Holy! Holy! Holy is the Lord God Almighty, Who was and is, and Who shall be forever!"

Dozens upon dozens danced, leaping and twirling before the only Begotten Son of God. The glory and honor grew brighter as the dancing and songs of praise continued, but not long enough—never long enough.

Strolling forward, Jesus passed into God's Glory.

Dodi and Namrel followed. The cherub fell to his knees and continued to extoll the Lord's greatness and mercy.

All of heaven lined up, side by side, and created a path straight to God's throne. They, too, praised Jesus, singing of His greatness and great Love as He walked to His Father.

Approaching near to the great I AM, though not too close, Dodi fell to his knees and worshiped.

WELL DONE MY SON
COME SIT AT MY RIGHT HAND UNTIL I MAKE
YOUR EMEMIES YOUR FOOTSTOOL

Scriptures of Interest

. . . from King James Version

These are the verses that helped to 'fill in' God's story of those precious and most important days—the three days Jesus did not spend in the tomb. Please look at them for yourselves, and if you discover any scripture— here or in the Word—that indicates in anyway it doesn't fit or changes God's story, please contact the publisher.
P,O. Box 622 Clarksville, Texas 75426

Chapter One

Matthew 1

[18] Now the birth of Jesus Christ was on this wise: When as his mother Mary was espoused to Joseph, before they came together, she was found with child of the Holy Ghost.

[19] Then Joseph her husband, being a just man, and not willing to make her a public example, was minded to put her away privily.

[20] But while he thought on these things, behold, the angel of the LORD appeared unto him in a dream, saying, Joseph, thou son of David, fear not to take unto thee Mary thy wife: for that which is conceived in her is of the Holy Ghost.

Luke 2

[3] And all went to be taxed, every one into his own city.

[4] And Joseph also went up from Galilee, out of the city of Nazareth, into Judaea, unto the city of David, which is called Bethlehem; (because he was of the house and lineage of David:)

[5] To be taxed with Mary his espoused wife, being great with child.

Luke 2

[13] And suddenly there was with the angel a multitude of the heavenly host praising God, and saying,

¹⁴ Glory to God in the highest, and on earth peace, good will toward men.

Matthew 2:13

And when they were departed, behold, the angel of the Lord appeareth to Joseph in a dream, saying, Arise, and take the young child and his mother,
and flee into Egypt, and be thou there until I bring thee word: for Herod will seek the young child to destroy him.

Matthew 2:16

Then Herod, when he saw that he was mocked of the wise men, was exceeding wroth, and sent forth, and slew all the children that were in Bethlehem, and in all the coasts thereof, from two years old and under, according to the time which he had diligently inquired of the wise men.

Chapter Two

Isaiah 14

[12] How art thou fallen from heaven, O Lucifer, son of the morning! How art thou cut down to the ground, which didst weaken the nations!

[13] For thou hast said in thine heart, I will ascend into heaven, I will exalt my throne above the stars of God: I will sit also upon the mount of the congregation, in the sides of the north:

[14] I will ascend above the heights of the clouds; I will be like the Most High.

Revelation 5:13

And every creature which is in heaven, and on the earth, and under the earth, and such as are in the sea, and all that are in them, heard I saying, Blessing, and honour, and glory, and power, be unto him that sitteth upon the throne, and unto the Lamb for ever and ever.

Chapter Three

Luke 4

[28] And all they in the synagogue, when they heard these things, were filled with wrath,

[29] And rose up, and thrust him out of the city, and led him unto the brow of the hill whereon their city was built, that they might cast him down headlong.

[30] But he passing through the midst of them went his way,

John 10

[33] The Jews answered him, saying, For a good work we stone thee not; but for blasphemy; and because that thou, being a man, makest thyself God.

[34] Jesus answered them, Is it not written in your law, I said, Ye are gods? [35] If he called them gods, unto whom the word of God came, and the scripture cannot be broken;

[36] Say ye of him, whom the Father hath sanctified, and sent into the world, Thou blasphemest; because I said, I am the Son of God?

[37] If I do not the works of my Father, believe me not. [38] But if I do, though ye believe not me, believe the works: that ye may know, and believe, that the Father is in me, and I in him.

[39] Therefore they sought again to take him: but he escaped out of their hand,

Isaiah 53

⁴ Surely he hath borne our griefs, and carried our sorrows: yet we did esteem him stricken, smitten of God, and afflicted.

⁵ But he was wounded for our transgressions, he was bruised for our iniquities: the chastisement of our peace was upon him; and with his stripes we are healed.

⁶ All we like sheep have gone astray; we have turned every one to his own way; and the LORD hath laid on him the iniquity of us all.

John 12

³¹ Now is the judgment of this world: now shall the prince of this world be cast out.

Isaiah 50

⁶ I gave my back to the smiters, and my cheeks to them that plucked off the hair: I hid not my face from shame and spitting.

⁷ For the Lord GOD will help me; therefore shall I not be confounded: therefore have I set my face like a flint, and I know that I shall not be ashamed.

Isaiah 6:10

Make the heart of this people fat, and make their ears heavy, and shut their eyes; lest they see with their eyes, and hear with their ears, and understand with their heart, and convert, and be healed.

Matthew 27:32

And as they came out, they found a man of Cyrene, Simon by name: him they compelled to bear his cross.

Luke 2:43

And Jesus said unto him, Verily I say unto thee, Today shalt thou be with me in paradise.

Mark 15

33 And when the sixth hour was come, there was darkness over the whole land until the ninth hour.

34 And at the ninth hour Jesus cried with a loud voice, saying, Eloi, Eloi, lama sabachthani? Which is, being interpreted, My God, my God, why hast thou forsaken me?

John 19

28 After this, Jesus knowing that all things were now accomplished, that the scripture might be fulfilled, saith, I thirst.

29 Now there was set a vessel full of vinegar: and they filled a spunge with vinegar, and put it upon hyssop, and put it to his mouth.

30 When Jesus therefore had received the vinegar, he said, It is finished: and he bowed his head, and gave up the ghost.

Chapter Four

Psalm 119:105
Thy word is a lamp unto my feet, and a light unto my path.

Hebrew 12:1
Wherefore seeing we also are compassed about with so great a cloud of witnesses,

Isaiah 53:12
Therefore will I divide him a portion with the great, and he shall divide the spoil with the strong; because he hath poured out his soul unto death: and he was numbered with the transgressors; and he bare the sin of many and made intercession for the transgressors.

Deuteronomy 25:1
If there be a controversy between men, and they come unto judgment, that the judges may judge them; then they shall justify the righteous and condemn the wicked.

Hebrews 9:27
And as it is appointed unto men once to die, but after this the judgment:

Chapter Five

John 11

[25]Jesus said unto her, I am the resurrection, and the life: he that believeth in me, though he were dead, yet shall he live:

[26]And whosoever liveth and believeth in me shall never die. Believest thou this? [27]She saith unto him, Yea, Lord: I believe that thou art the Christ, the Son of God, which should come into the world.

[28]And when she had so said, she went her way, and called Mary her sister secretly, saying, The Master is come, and calleth for thee.

[29]As soon as she heard that, she arose quickly, and came unto him. [30]Now Jesus was not yet come into the town but was in that place where Martha met him.

Exodus 20:10

But the seventh day is the sabbath of the LORD thy God: in it thou shalt not do any work, thou, nor thy son, nor thy daughter, thy manservant, nor thy maidservant, nor thy cattle, nor thy stranger that is within thy gates:

Exodus 35:3

Ye shall kindle no fire throughout your habitations upon the sabbath day.

Leviticus 25:4

But in the seventh year shall be a sabbath of rest unto the land, a sabbath for the LORD: thou shalt neither sow thy field, nor prune thy vineyard.

Numbers 15

[32] And while the children of Israel were in the wilderness, they found a man that gathered sticks upon the sabbath day.

[33] And they that found him gathering sticks brought him unto Moses and Aaron, and unto all the congregation. [34] And they put him in ward, because it was not declared what should be done to him.

[35] And the LORD said unto Moses, The man shall be surely put to death: all the congregation shall stone him with stones without the camp.

Matthew 12

[1] At that time Jesus went on the sabbath day through the corn; and his disciples were an hungered, and began to pluck the ears of corn and to eat.

[10] And, behold, there was a man which had his hand withered. And they asked him, saying, Is it lawful to heal on the sabbath days? That they might accuse him.

[11] And he said unto them, What man shall there be among you, that shall have one sheep, and if it fall into a pit on the sabbath day, will he not lay hold on it, and lift it out?

¹² How much then is a man better than a sheep? Wherefore it is lawful to do well on the sabbath days.

¹³ Then saith he to the man, Stretch forth thine hand. And he stretched it forth; and it was restored whole, like as the other.

Deuteronomy 23:25

When thou comest into the standing corn of thy neighbor, then thou mayest pluck the ears with thine hand; but thou shalt not move a sickle unto thy neighbor's standing corn.

Author's note—proof that He did not break the Law of the Sabbath when His disciples plucked and ate the corn.

Chapter Six

Exodus 20:12

Honour thy father and thy mother: that thy days may be long upon the land which the LORD thy God giveth thee.

Author's note—Satan accused Him of not honoring His earthly parents as well as His Heavenly Father.

Luke 2

⁴²And when he was twelve years old, they went up to Jerusalem after the custom of the feast.

⁴³And when they had fulfilled the days, as they returned, the child Jesus tarried behind in Jerusalem; and Joseph and his mother knew not of it.

⁴⁴ But they, supposing him to have been in the company, went a day's journey; and they sought him among their kinsfolk and acquaintance.

⁴⁵And when they found him not, they turned back again to Jerusalem, seeking him.

⁴⁶And it came to pass, that after three days they found him in the temple, sitting in the midst of the doctors, both hearing them, and asking them questions.

⁴⁷And all that heard him were astonished at his understanding and answers.

⁴⁸And when they saw him, they were amazed: and his mother said unto him, Son, why hast thou thus dealt

with us? Behold, thy father and I have sought thee sorrowing.

⁴⁹And he said unto them, How is it that ye sought me? Wist ye not that I must be about my Father's business?

John 6

³⁵And Jesus said unto them, I am the bread of life: he that cometh to me shall never hunger; and he that believeth on me shall never thirst.

³⁶But I said unto you, That ye also have seen me, and believe not. ³⁷All that the Father giveth me shall come to me; and him that cometh to me I will in no wise cast out.

³⁸For I came down from heaven, not to do mine own will, but the will of him that sent me.

³⁹And this is the Father's will which hath sent me, that of all which he hath given me I should lose nothing but should raise it up again at the last day.

⁴⁰And this is the will of him that sent me, that everyone which seeth the Son, and believeth on him, may have everlasting life: and I will raise him up at the last day.

Psalm 69:9

For the zeal of thine house hath eaten me up; and the reproaches of them that reproached thee are fallen upon me.

Author's note—This is from when Jesus was twelve and stayed behind at the temple. He wanted His Father's house to be holy from His early age.

Revelation 1:18

I am he that liveth and was dead; and behold, I am alive for evermore, Amen; and have the keys of hell and of death.

Luke 20

[35] But they which shall be accounted worthy to obtain that world, and the resurrection from the dead, neither marry, nor are given in marriage:

[36] Neither can they die any more: for they are equal unto the angels; and are the children of God, being the children of the resurrection.

Matthew 11:28

Come unto me, all ye that labour and are heavy laden, and I will give you rest.

Chapter Seven

Zechariah 3

³Now Joshua was clothed with filthy garments and stood before the angel. ⁴ And he answered and spake unto those that stood before him, saying, Take away the filthy garments from him.

Isaiah 61:1

The Spirit of the Lord GOD is upon me; because the LORD hath anointed me to preach good tidings unto the meek; he hath sent me to bind up the brokenhearted, to proclaim liberty to the captives, and the opening of the prison to them that are bound;

Author's note—I believe this verse applies also to those who love and follow Christ on earth as well as Jesus Himself. Those in Paradise and Torment were captives, separated from Father God by their sins. As of then, they had no Savior.

Psalm 16

⁹ Therefore my heart is glad, and my glory rejoiceth: my flesh also shall rest in hope. ¹⁰ For thou wilt not leave my soul in hell; neither wilt thou suffer thine Holy One to see corruption.

Author's note—another scripture that tells me Jesus preached the Good News to those in Torment.

Chapter Eight

Luke 24

¹Now upon the first day of the week, very early in the morning, they came unto the sepulchre, bringing the spices which they had prepared, and certain others with them.

²And they found the stone rolled away from the sepulcher. ³And they entered in and found not the body of the Lord Jesus.

⁴And it came to pass, as they were much perplexed thereabout, behold, two men stood by them in shining garments:

⁵And as they were afraid, and bowed down their faces to the earth, they said unto them, Why seek ye the living among the dead?

⁶He is not here but is risen: remember how he spake unto you when he was yet in Galilee,

⁷Saying, The Son of man must be delivered into the hands of sinful men, and be crucified, and the third day rise again.

Ephesians 4

⁹(Now that he ascended, what is it but that he also descended first into the lower parts of the earth? ¹⁰He that descended is the same also that ascended up far above all heavens, that he might fill all things.)

Author's note—This and other Scriptures brought

me to the conclusion that Jesus descended into Hades to share the Good News and take back the keys of death and hell. *Revelation 1:18* I am he that liveth and was dead; and behold, I am alive for evermore, Amen; and have the keys of hell and of death.

If Jesus died for ALL, to cover all the sins of the world so that those who believed could be saved, then He died for the worst of men in Torment. They hadn't had the opportunity to accept or reject His gift of salvation.

Psalm 110:10

The LORD said unto my Lord, Sit thou at my right hand, until I make thine enemies thy footstool.

Author's note—For years, we talked about writing THEN JUDGMENT, but how can one get into the Lord's head and heart as we endeavor to do with all our characters in our works of fiction? It's necessary to have a 'point of view' to bring our readers right down into the story to walk with those who populate our books.

We weren't comfortable to do that for Jesus. The Way made a way! We could use Dodi to tell the story! As always in our Biblical fiction, we are dedicated not to stray from God's own story—His living Word.

My husband Ron grew up in the Church of Christ, while I went to a Baptist congregation. Hopefully, neither of these—nor any other denominations' secular teachings—have crept into this story.

There are just a few verses in the Bible regarding angels. Using those clues, we've imagined the cherubim were created first, that there are seventy-two of them, and that they keep three "watches" of twenty-four.

One of those divisions of elders are always before God's throne, praising the beauty of His Holiness, casting their crowns at His feet.

In our story, when the watch changes, to Namrel and his brothers serving before the throne, it seems they had only just arrived—no matter how many star twinklings have passed.

The hosts lift the cherubim onto the backs of the seraphim who fly them to the Temple made without hands where they remain, serving a second watch, until God's glory clinging to them returns to Him.

The Father of Lights is jealous of His Glory.

Again, it seems like only a short period. For their third watch, they have an away interlude to pursue their own interests, still doing the will of the Father, of course, until the next change of the watch.

Before God's throne, they are renewed and refreshed. When they leave Heaven's Temple, they are as when first created.

The host of heaven, we imagined, were at first created the size of the cherubim, but as God spewed each new one from His mind into the Crystal Sea, they became larger and more powerful, according to God's purpose.

Dodi was the last and most awesome of that brotherhood.

The triplet archangels, Gabriel, Michael, and Lucifer were created next, able to stand before the Almighty. As his calling card, God's messenger told Zacharias that he could.

And the angel answering said unto him, I am Gabriel, that stands in the presence of God; and am sent to speak unto thee, and to shew thee these glad tidings. Luke 1:19

We believe the other two can also stand in God's presence.

In our Biblical fiction series, **The Generations**, there's more on how the angels war and their lives in Heaven as we've come to believe. Each book, presenting Adam, Noah, and Abraham as its main character, respectively, covers all the rest between and up to them.

Each of those stories also has a "Scriptures of Interest" section for you to consider.

In them, Dodi, last of the host, had not yet chosen a name, but was called Centurion as the captain over a hundred.

We had great fun meeting and writing about Namrel, first of the cherubim. He became so real to us we'll surely be surprised if he doesn't greet us one day in Heaven.

If you are not a believer, we pray that you will fall to your knees and ask Jesus to forgive you and save your soul—a gift He freely gives.

If you have any questions or concerns regarding our beliefs, please feel free to email me at Caryl.McAdoo@yahoo.com —I love hearing from readers!

Please be a blessing and take the time to review this book while it's fresh on your mind. Or if you prefer, after you've pondered and considered.

Replenish the Earth
Volume Three

Children of Eber
Volume Four

OTHERS

I AM My Beloved

    And now . . . please enjoy a SNEAK PEEK of
Caryl's next historical romance JO, her 2022
contribution to The Fourth Annual Prairie Roses
Collection, book 23! These stories feature strong
women who journey in a covered wagon. JO launches
May 3, 2022, on Caryl's birthday!

March 15th 1840
Five miles outside of Memphis, Tennessee

The wagon rounded a curve. Right there on the side of the road, a herd of goats nibbled on the little trees and grass and weeds along the fence. "Pa, can I have a kid of my own?"

"You'll have to ask your Papa, Jo. The goats belong to him and Mima."

"A kid is a lot of responsibility, honey. Maybe when you're older."

Jolene looked from her father to her mother. "But I'm six now! I'll take good care of her. She can sleep with me. Please, Ma?"

"Sweetheart, your father said to ask Papa."

"All right, I will! And if he says yes, then I can have one? How much further is it, Pa?"

"A mile or so. Their place is just around the next bend in the road. How about being quiet for a while?"

Not talk? That was so hard. It'd been a long trip, and she'd tried, but there was so much she wanted to know, especially after hearing that very morning about the royal wedding happening just after Pa loaded her and Ma up in the buggy and got on the way! A new question just burned its way out.

"How come Queen Victoria got to marry her cousin? I thought that was against the rules. Don't they have to follow the same rules as us?"

"Not really, sweetie, but I don't think they're first cousins. Second or third cousins aren't as bad."

"What number cousins are Queen Victoria and Price Albert? Why do they still call him prince? Isn't he a king if he's married to the queen? It just doesn't' seem right—her being queen and him only a prince."

"Shhh. I'm not sure, baby. Maybe Mima will know."

"Is that because she and Papa came from England?"

"I don't know, honey, but they did come from England. Remember your father asked you to be quiet."

"Yes, ma'am. I will." She met her father's stern eyes and smiled. "Can we go to England someday? I'd love to see the Queen."

"What about your goat? If Papa gives you one, who would take care of him while we went off to England? It's a very long way away across the ocean."

"Well, she could visit her mother while we were gone, couldn't she? So can we go? It's still my birthday week! Can we go for my birthday? Please?"

A pop sounded. "What was that?"

"It sounded like a gun." Pa slapped the reins over the horse's rump.

"A gun? But why . . ."

The buggy rounded the bend in the road and then turned off toward the house set back in the trees just as another pop sounded. That one louder.

"That was gunshot. What in the world—"

"Oh, hurry, Thomas!" Her mother's voice was scary. "Get under the seat, baby! Right now! Cover up with the blanket. Cover your head, too, and don't make a sound or move at all until I come get you. Do you understand?"

The horse was going so fast. It slung her one way then the other.

"Yes, Ma." Jolene scurried under the seat and blanket as fast as she could. Her heart bumped against her chest so hard. Ma helped get her all covered up.

"Stay there! Don't come out!"

What was happening? "Yes ma'am." Why was someone shooting at Mima and Papa's? Why was her Pa driving so fast and her mother so afraid? She filled her lungs with the stale air under the blanket but need more air. She uncovered her face and gulped another breath.

"Jolene Mae! Don't uncover even your face! Be perfectly still. Do you hear?"

The buggy came to a stop, and she could tell Pa jumped down by the shaking on his side, then her mother's side shook, too. The door slammed. Papa hated anyone slamming the door. She was always careful to hold it until it shut so he wouldn't get on to her in that voice he used when he was angry.

Pa hollered loud. Another gunshot sounded. It was so loud, it made her jump, but she had to be still.

Ma screamed his name. Then another boom. Her body jerked again a little, but she stayed as still as she could.

Jolene's heart pounded. Her breath came hard.

What had happened?

Was it Papa shooting?

It got so quiet. She lay still as she could. She hope her mother would hurry up. Where was she? Why didn't she come?

Someone went up the porch stairs then in a little bit, another person. Was it Ma and Pa? Did they go in the house? Did they forget her? No. Ma wouldn't never do that. Everything inside her wanted to lift that blanket and peek, but she didn't dare. Why was it so quiet? She lay very still. After a bit, her eyes grew so heavy. She tried to keep them open, but she just had to rest them.

Why weren't her parents coming to get her?

Josiah turned off the road. At the sight of Thomas' buggy, his heart soared.

"Well, bless God! He decided to come early."

But . . . Had they just got there?

Why was the horse still hitched up?

Where was his little Jolene?

The tree swing hung still.

Pulling past his son's rig, he gasped. His daughter-in-law lay face down on the ground. What in the world—?

His mind reeled at the carnage. A bit ahead of Madeline, his son sprawled across the porch steps, his leg at an odd angle. His throat went dry.

What had happened?

His eyes couldn't be right. They were . . . his brain refused the thought.

"God! God! Father God—"

It couldn't be.

Ilene! Where was his wife? Had she seen them?

Running past Thomas, he stepped through the door. The room looked normal, but it wasn't. The house was too quiet. He called out.

"Ilene? Where are you?" He stepped across the hardwood floor, his boots on them reverberating in the silence. It proved difficult to put one foot in front of the other.

His heart raced. Why didn't she answer?

"Ilene?" He stepped into the kitchen. Mis'ess Hood, the neighbor lady, lay on the floor. Blood stained the bodice of her dress. A pool of the dark redness had pooled beside her. "Oh, Lord! No!"

Where was Ilene? He found his wife in the bedroom, a big hole in her chest. The mattress covered her feet. Drawers pulled out of the dresser lay scattered about.

He went numb.

How could it be?

In a stupor of disbelief, he placed the mattress back on its frame before lifting his wife onto it then placed a pillow under her head. He leaned over her and kissed her forehead.

Thomas. He had to get his son and daughter-in-law. He dragged his boy into his old room then struggled to get him up on the bed. Next, Madeline. He lifted the lifeless body of his daughter-in-law and carried her to lay beside her husband.

Oh, Lord. How? Why? His eyes teared and blurred his sight. He sank to his knees.

Who had done it?

What monster killed his family?

And why? He'd stowed away a bit of savings, but nothing to cause a thief to . . . More tears welled, and he wept. Amidst his sobs, a thought hit him hard. Jo! Where was his little Jolene?

Jumping to his feet, he hurried back outside. "Jo? Jolene! Where are you, baby? It's your papa! You can come out now."

Nothing moved. Only the leaves in the trees rustled in the breeze. The buggy! That's why the horse was still tied up! He ran to it. "Jo? Where are you, baby girl? It's Papa." First thing, he spotted the little bundle under the seat. Very slightly, it moved up and down. She was breathing! He pulled back the blanket, uncovering the angelic sleeping face of his granddaughter.

Little golden curls fell over her forehead and cheek. He straightened one then scooped her into his arms. "Little angel. Papa's angel." He hugged her to himself and rocked her.

"Papa? I took a nap because I had to be so still. Where's Ma?" She stretched her arms toward the sky. "Does Mima have cookies? Can I have my own baby goat? Do you know why Prince Albert isn't the king now?"

"Oh, my baby girl. A terrible thing has happened."

More grief and sorrow than any child should bear fell upon Jolene. Poor child. Days passed by like a parade clown. Perhaps not soon enough, or maybe too soon, the dear girl embraced a new reality. While she would always miss them all, her mother visiting her dreams lessened the pain in her little chest.

That and her grandfather and everyone at church reassuring her Mima and her parents lived in Heaven and were waiting for her.

The days piled upon themselves.

Uncle Abe, her Papa's younger brother, came to help, then Miss Hattie hired on to cook and keep house. No doubt, Mima would have approved.

Josiah met Rabbi Simon Goldman who came to the farm each quarter to supervise making the special Torah parchment. The business expanded to new heights. More goats were bought, and to all's surprise, Jolene had a God given talent for calligraphy. By twelve, her birth and marriage certificates were in high demand, fetching a princely price.

Abe convinced his brother to expand the goat herd, breeding only the best milkers. Each day, the does produced over twenty gallons of milk that two milkmen came and hauled off. The bottom line looked very nice, quiet high actually.

If only Josiah could catch his breath on muggy days, things would be wonderful for the old widower. He expected—and hoped more as Jolene grew—to join his wife, son, and daughter-in-law sooner before later.

A new doctor hung out his shingle in Memphis, and Jolene—she heard about him at church—finally convinced her grandfather to pay the man a visit.

February 22, 1850
Halfway from Memphis to the Foster Farm

"Oh, Papa! Will you please stop arguing with me and listen to reason? We have to. What would I do if anything happened to you?" Jolene patted the old darling's knee. "Come on. It'll be an adventure. We love those, don't we?"

"Long as they're close to home, I guess we do." He flicked the reins over the gelding's back, and the horse broke into a trot. The fence line whizzed by. "But it's crazy-thinking. We can't just pack up and move across the county, Jo. It'll be fine. I can still catch a breath."

Turning sideways in the buggy seat, she rubbed her brow. What could she say to convince him? He had to give way to good sense. "You heard him just as well as I did. The air is just so heavy with moisture here. That's why you can't breathe sometimes, but if we move to Santa Fe, you won't have near as much trouble."

A coughing fit took him over then he wheezed, gasping for air before he shook his head. "No, ma'am. I'm not doing it. Our family is buried here. We can't run off and leave them."

"But they aren't, are they? Haven't you told me these past ten years how they're in Heaven waiting for us? Papa, I'm not ready for you to join them."

"Don't you worry, that's a long way off yet. What about our goats? You have certificates to make. Besides, what would the milkmen do if we moved?"

"Well, we could sell them some of the goats. That'll make them happy, don't you think? We will take the best bucks and does with us. There's no reason we can't keep right on making parchment once we get there and get settled. The business may even be better in Santa Fe."

"Rabbi Simon is coming next week. I like sleeping in my own bed in my own house, granddaughter. I'm too old to be traipsing across country and trying to make a new start. I can't build another house. Now drop it. I'll be fine."

"With all due respect, sir, no! I can't because you aren't fine, are you. Do you not hear yourself wheezing with almost every breath? Doc Mansville says moving to the desert will add years to your life. Just you wait and see how good you'll feel, how much better you breathe."

"That old saw bones ain't that sharp, Jo. He doesn't know that. How could he?" He turned off the road.

"It's science, Papa. Desert air is so much dryer there, so the air's thinner. It's easier to breathe for anyone. Think how good it will be for me."

"I appreciate that, darlin', but I got years to live right here."

"We've just got to take some time to figure out what all need to be done before we go. We just can't stay here."

"Now shush about all that nonsense. Shouldn't have ever even let you talk me into going to see that old quack anyway. Now come on, Jolene. We have work to do."

"What work? As far as I'm concerned, there's nothing more important than this conversation. You know it isn't nonsense. You know Doc is right, so I won't hush. I can't. Someway, I have to get through to you. You are all I have in the world, and it hurts my heart when you can't breathe. What would I do without you, Papa. I never want to find out."

"You're making a mountain out of a molehill, little girl."

Her heart fell. "I'm not. Will you at least promise me you'll think about it? I want you to go on inside and take a load off. I'll help Uncle Abe with the milking and feeding. You just head on in and boss Miss Hattie around while she cooks our supper." She play punched his shoulder. "You know she's sweet on you."

"Daughter, hush. You're Mima will rollover in her grave, you talking like that."

"Oh, Papa. She wouldn't care one bit. I have no doubt, not one, that she'd want you to have a happy life. There's nothing wrong with you having a lady friend. Remember what they say at weddings . . . until death do us part. Did you and Mima say that?"

"Gracious, child, that was over forty-five years ago. How can I remember exactly what was said?" He reined the horse to a stop inside the barn. "I'm sixty-four, and I don't need or want a lady friend. For sure not that old Russian. I can hardly understand her half the time."

Jolene laughed. "That's only because you're getting so hard of hearing. I wonder if the desert air would help your hearing, too." She jumped down, giggling, and ran to the other side. She extended her hand. "Here, Papa. Now please, do as I ask. Go inside and get comfortable and set your mind to thinking what all we need to do before we leave. Make a list. Miss Hattie can fetch paper and ink."

"You sure are bossy." He let her help him down then paused a minute before he took two big breaths. "What about Buford Maxwell?"

"What about him?"

"Thought you set your bonnet for the young man?"

"Oh, Papa, that was two years ago. He's such a boy. If I ever do marry, you can write it in stone I'll be hitching my star to a mature, grownup man." She patted his chest. "Someone like my best friend and grandest grandfather."

As in his usual fashion, he held one arm out. She snuggled into his chest and helped him to the house. Once inside, she held his hand, easing him down into his rocker.

"Need a glass of water or anything before I get busy?"

"Not a thing. You go on. Miss Hattie can fetch for me if I need anything."

Speaking of the lady, she appeared in the doorway, drying her hands on her apron. "Not unless you say please, I won't, you old codger."

"Say please and flip you some gold, huh?" He chuckled.

"I'll be in the barn, Miss Hattie." Jolene headed outside, but turned and stuck her head back in. "Could you get him some paper and ink for me? He needs to make a list." She smiled as she turned and quietly closed the screen door.

"A leest you need to make, huh? What's going on that leest of yours, Mister Foster? If I may ask, that is."

JO debuts May 3, 2022, it's author's birthday! It's available on Amazon now for pre-orders. Get yours today!

Coming Soon Titles

Some of these titles, those without release dates, are planned or started, but not complete yet. God's will be done.

Historical

Prairie Roses Collection
Jo   1850   book twenty-three   May 2022

Cross Timber Romance Family Saga
Texas Twosome, 1870s   book nine   September 2022

Wagons West Romances
1849 – Gold Rushers   book one   ???

Texas Romance Companions

The Revivalist Trilogy
   King David's Tabernacle   book three   ???

Contemporary Romance

The Pitch   ???

King of Texas, starring Patrick Henry Buckmeyer III

Biblical Fiction – The Prophets Collection

Jeremiah   book one   ???

Mystery

Prophetic Justice   ???

All of Caryl's Books

Historical Christian Romance

Texas Romance Family Saga Series

Vow Unbroken, Prelude 1832
Hearts Stolen, Book One 1839-1844
Hope Reborn, Book Two 1850-51
Sins of the Mothers, Book Three 1851-53
Daughters of the Heart, Book Four 1853-54
Just Kin, Book Five 1861-65
At Liberty to Love, Book Six 1865-66
Covering Love, Book Seven 1885-86
Mighty to Save, Book Eight 1918-1924
Chief of Sinners, Book Nine 1826-1951

Texas Romance Companion Books

The Bedwarmer's Son, 1859 & 1926
Son of Promise, 1950   (Cody Buckmeyer at twelve)
Bipartisan Love, 1968 (Cody Buckmeyer at thirty)
Jewel's Gold, 1895
      The Revivalist Trilogy
John David's Calling, Book One 1968-70
Hannah Claire's Wilderness, Book Two 1971
Sing a New Song, contemporary

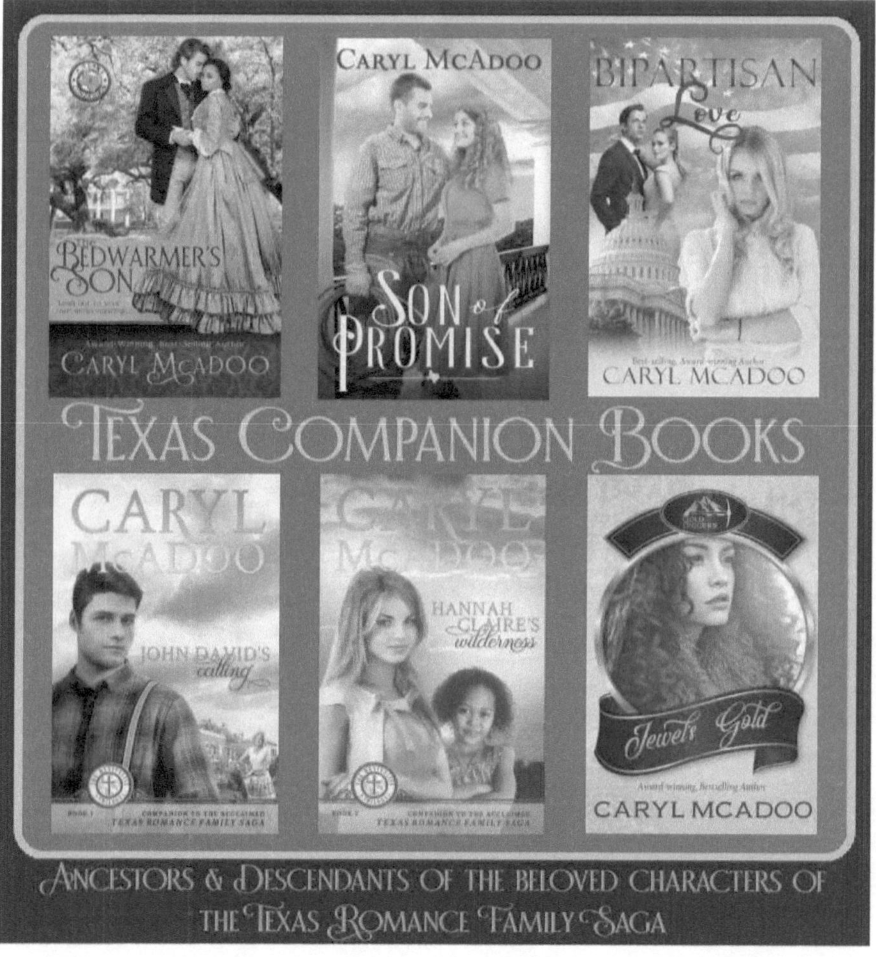

CROSS TIMBER ROMANCES FAMILY SAGA

Gone to Texas, Book One 1840
Texas My Texas, Book Two 1841
Texas Tears, Book Three 1845
Leaving Texas, Book Four 1850
Texas Troubles, Book Five 1860
Texas Trails, Book Six 1869

Thanksgiving Books & Blessings Collection

Gone to Texas, Texas Tears, & Texas Troubles, Texas Timbers (all above)

Cross Timbers Companion Books

QUINCY & PRISCILLA at The Lowell House, 1866, book one

Cross Timbers Romantic Mystery

Book One DUPLICITY at The Lowell House
Book Two SKULLDUGGERY in the Sulphur River Bottoms
Book Three COERCION at The Cow Palace

Lockets & Lace

Silent Harmony 1867   Uniquely Common 1852   Bitter Honey 1857

Prairie Roses

Remi 1853   Lilah 1855   Ruth 1842   Jo 1849

North & South; Civil War Brides
Kentucky Bride
1861

Nursing the Heart
A Nurse for Jacob
1868

Contemporary Romance

Red River Romances

The Preacher's Faith
Sing a New Song
One and Done

Apple Orchard Romances
Lady Luck's a Loser

Mid-Grade / Young Adult

River Bottom Ranch Stories

The Adventures of Sergeant Socks: The Journey Home, Book1
The Adventures of Sergeant Socks: The Bravest Heart, Book 2
Amazing Graci, Guardian of the River Bottom Goats, Book 3

Days of Dread Trilogy

The King's Highway, Book One
The Sixth Trumpet, Book Two
The Kidron Valley, Book Three

Non-fiction

Great Firehouse Cooks of Texas
Antiquing in North Texas (out-of-date
Story & Style, The Craft of Writing Creative Fiction
Heart"wings" Devotional

Miscellaneous Novels

The Thief of Dreams (**not for Christian market**!)
The Price Paid, hard cover (based on WWII true story)
Absolute Pi (audio; mystery)
Apple Orchard B&B, hard cover (re-released as Lady Luck's a Loser)

ℛEACH OUT TO YOUR AUTHOR

Author Pages : *(please follow)*
Amazon   http://tinyurl.com/CarylsAmazonAuthorPage

BookBub   https://www.bookbub.com/authors/caryl-mcadoo?follow=true

Simon & Schuster   http://tinyurl.com/S-SCarylsPage

Website   http://www.CarylMcAdoo.com

Newsletter   http://tinyurl.com/TheCaryler

YouTube   http://bit.ly/2qGJoToBlog *(Caryl's new songs!)*

Blogs   http://www.CarylMcAdoo.blogspot.com
                    Heart"wings" Blog

Facebook   http://www.facebook.com/CarylMcAdoo.author

Twitter   http://www.twitter.com/CarylMcAdoo

GoodReads http://tinyurl.com/GoodReadsCaryl

Google+   http://tinyurl.com/CarylsGooglePlus

Pinterest   http://www.pinterest.com/CarylMcAdoo

LinkedIn   http://www.linkedIn.com/CarylMcAdoo

Email   CarylMcAdoo@yahoo.com

Author Reaching Out to You

Hey dear Readers!

What a blessing and gift from God you are! I'm so grateful that you read my stories and love them and review them! I pray you found THEN JUDGMENT gave God glory.

My desire is that each one of my stories brings you closer to Him, encourages you, and offers scriptural principles to give you a few life issues to ponder I try to include things He's taught me from His Word—things that make my life easier and better!

I could use your help in spreading the word of my Kingdom novels. To stay on top of all my book news (debuts, sales, awards), I encourage you to subscribe to *The Caryler*, my newsletter. I try to make it fun with news, scripture, lyrics, including a few of my favorite things.

Speaking of lyrics, I'm blessed that God gives me new songs! There's nothing I love more than praising and worshiping Him. Now you can hear a few of the songs at my YouTube channel! Please subscribe so you won't miss any!

Reviews are so important to authors, so it'll be a **big boon** if you could take the time to leave a quick review. It doesn't have to be long at Amazon, Goodreads, BookBub, your blog, and anywhere you enjoy reading about books. Click "Follow" while you're there, too! ☺

Of course, tell your friends—word of mouth is invaluable!

I love hearing from you and have a group of special readers who help me more than most. Let me know if you'd like to join my street team's Facebook group, Carylers Choir review crew.

Stop by my Facebook page; I just love connecting! Just search Caryl McAdoo. And last but never least, I pray that God will bless you as you have blessed me, that His favor will envelope all you do!

Love in Christ and many blessings,

Caryl

FAVORITE PLACES

Needing help with your online presence?
Go to Rocksteady Marketing for websites and
email marketing assistance. Janis McAdoo
will be a God-sent blessing to you!

Subscribe to receive free and low-cost
Christian novels by email BookBub and The
Celebration Reading Room

Have a Book you want to Promote or Publish?
I highly recommend Celebrate Lit to help
promote your books! Great people!

Multi Author Collections (I'm a part of):
~ Prairie Roses
~ Lockets & Lace
~ Thanksgiving Books & Blessings

Facebook groups I love:
~ Christian Book Launches
~ Heart"Wings" Blog and More devotionals and ministry moments
~ Sweet Wild West Reads
~ Thanksgiving Books & Blessings for lovers of all things
Thanksgiving and clean, sweet, and Christian reading; an annual multi-
author collection!
~ Christian Indie Books great place to find books bargains and new
authors (sometimes even FREE)
~ Christian Indie Authors Readers Group another great place to meet
new authors and book deals (FREE, too, sometimes)
~ 5-Star Reviews of Christian Fiction: Find readers' favorites here!
Join and post your own reviews of books you love!
~ Celebrate Lit Community Forum Keep up with Christian fiction

~ Well Made Wellness Jessica will teach you how to walk in wellness with a whole heart. This encourager shares insights for well living, wholesome homes, and Bible roots to health and great recipes, covering ancestral, GAPS, paleo, and candida.

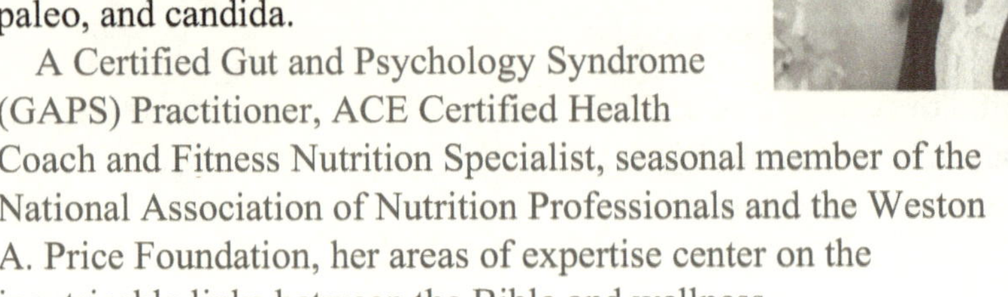

A Certified Gut and Psychology Syndrome (GAPS) Practitioner, ACE Certified Health Coach and Fitness Nutrition Specialist, seasonal member of the National Association of Nutrition Professionals and the Weston A. Price Foundation, her areas of expertise center on the inextricable links between the Bible and wellness

LOVE & BLESSINGS!